THE SMALL GARDEN
Written by
Giovanna Cicero

Illustrated and designed
by Alfonso Alaimo

Bumblebee Books
London

A CIP catalogue record for this title is
available from the British Library.

ISBN: 978-1-83934-533-3

Bumblebee Books is an imprint of
Olympia Publishers.

First Published in 2022

Bumblebee Books
Tallis House
2 Tallis Street
London
EC4Y 0AB

Printed in Great Britain

www.olympiapublishers.com

Dedication

I would like to dedicate this book firstly to my husband, Salvatore, who always encourages and supports me in whatever I do. Also to my two sons, Carlo and Reno, who always believe in me. And of course to Evie, my niece, who was the inspiration for me to write this book.

My name is Evie.

I am two-years-old, brown hair, two foot something with brown eyes and enjoy being outdoors.

As soon as I get up, I brush my teeth and get dressed as quickly as I can.

Daddy said, 'Come on, Evie. The quicker you eat breakfast the quicker you can go and play in the garden.'

It's a small garden but there so many things to see and do. Let me share my garden with you.

I look around the garden, what can I see?

I see... the olive tree.

It sits in the middle of the garden, very tall with silvery green leaves.

I look around the garden, what else can I see?

I see... the apple tree.

I pick the apples from the tree, so delicious and sweet, just like me.

I look around the garden, what else can I see?

I see... the cherry tree.

Yummy yum yum dark and mauve with a pip in the middle. You have to be careful when you eat them (make sure you remove the pip). One by one I put the cherries in my mouth.

I look around the garden, what else can I see?

I see... the bird bath.

The birds getting their feathers wet, splash splash they go, wetting their feathers in the water.

I look around the garden, what else can I see?

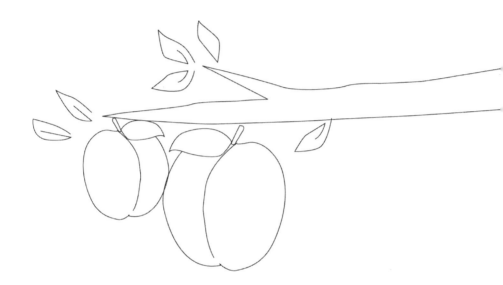

I see... the plum tree.

Dark purple fruit, you have to remove the stone before you eat it.

I look around the garden, what else can I see?

I see... the shed at the end of the garden.

That's where Daddy keeps all his potting pots.

I look around the garden, what else can I see?

I see... the bright red tomatoes.

Growing in their pots, just perfect and ready to eat.

I look around the garden, what else can I see?

I see... the lavender flower that stands up tall.

With my hands I touch them, they have a lovely smell.

I look around the garden, what else can I see?

I see... the garden mirror that hangs on the garden fence.

I can see me in the mirror looking back at me.

Look out for more
books in the series.

Mummy's Birthday Flowers

About the Author

Giovanna Cicero has worked in the bank industry for over thirty years, but watching her little niece exploring the garden in their North London home inspired her to write *Evie's Garden*. Her own pleasure in spending time in the garden, watching everything growing and changing with the seasons, motivated her to create her first children's book with Evie's help!

Acknowledgements

My brother, Alfonso Alaimo, who illustrated the book.
Without him it would never have come together. Jo Marcus,
who I would like to thank for her time and support.

Printed in Great Britain
by Amazon